Magical Mermaids
Activity Book

Becky J. Radtke

Dover Publications, Inc.
Mineola, New York

More than 30 enchanting activities all about mermaids will keep you entertained for hours. The fun-filled puzzles include word games, spot the differences, crosswords, mazes, secret codes, memory challenges, and more. You may even discover some things you never knew about these mythical sea creatures. So, grab a pencil and get started! You can check your answers in the Solutions section which starts on page 37. For added fun, color in the pictures any way you'd like.

Bibliographical Note

Magical Mermaids Activity Book is a new work,
first published by Dover Publications, Inc., in 2019.

International Standard Book Number
ISBN-13: 978-0-486-83653-9
ISBN-10: 0-486-83653-3

Manufactured in the United States by LSC Communications
83653301
www.doverpublications.com

2 4 6 8 10 9 7 5 3 1

2019

This mermaid is playing a magical tune that signals her ocean friends to come and play. Use the vowels in the bubbles to fill in the names of her special pals.

a e i o u

w h _ l _

s _ _ l

d _ l p h _ n

s t _ n g r _ y

t _ r t l _

l _ b s t _ r

Find and circle the one King Neptune that is different from the others.

Find and circle the hidden heart,
thumb, loaf of bread, pineapple, lips, feather duster,
sock, ladder, clown hat, and rose.

Use the picture clues to fill in the crossword. Some letters are included to give you a start.

3 Down

6 Across

4 Across

5 Down

1 Across

2 Down

Help these kids find their way to the dock to spot a mermaid before she disappears!

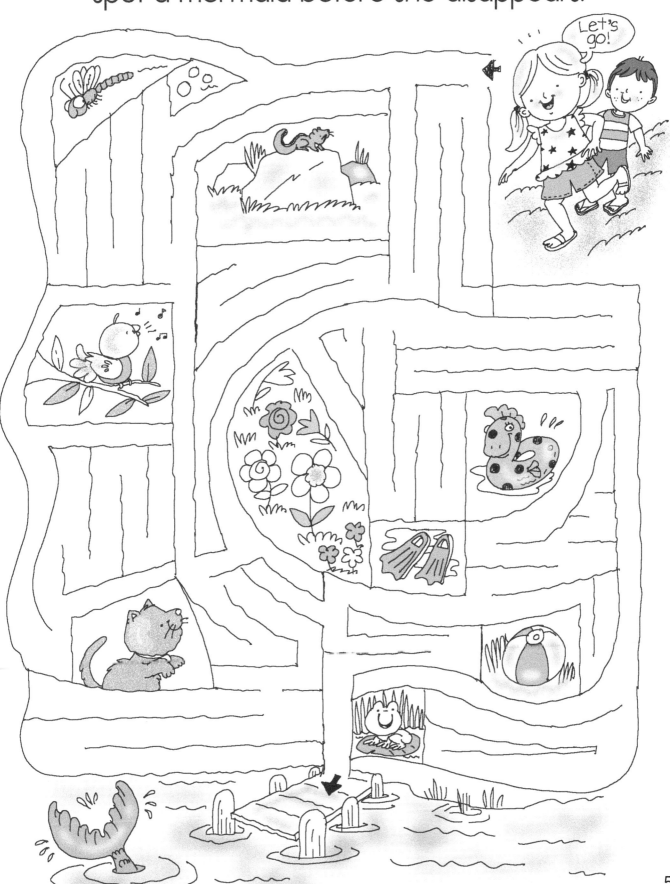

Use your imagination to create an original mermaid design on this tote bag.

The first syllable of mermaid is MER, which means "sea" in what language? Write the letter that comes before the one shown in each fish to spell the answer.

__ __ __ __ __ __

G S F O D I

Write the opposite of each word shown on the left. When you are done, print the letters in the squares from top to bottom on the nine blank lines below. They will spell out the name of a fish with a "heavenly" name.

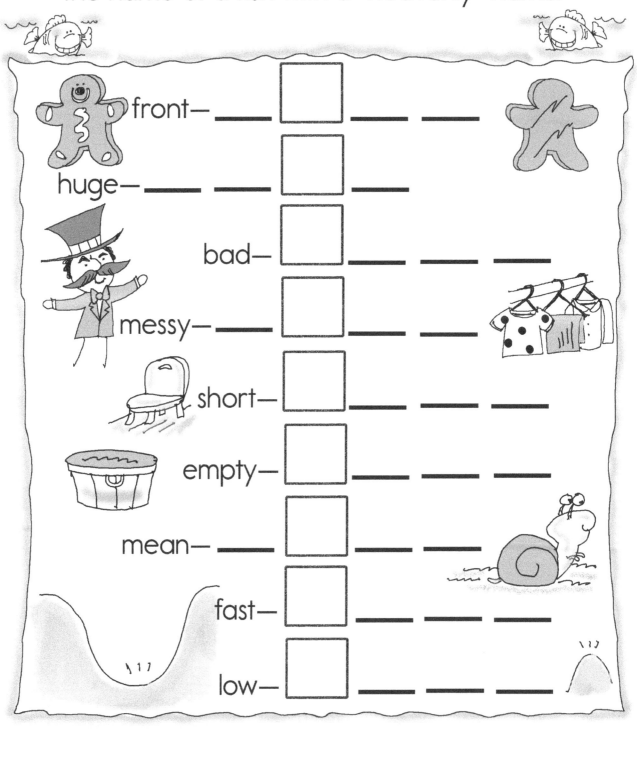

front— ___ [ ] ___ ___

huge— ___ ___ [ ] ___

bad— [ ] ___ ___ ___

messy— ___ [ ] ___ ___

short— [ ] ___ ___ ___

empty— [ ] ___ ___ ___

mean— ___ [ ] ___ ___

fast— [ ] ___ ___ ___

low— [ ] ___ ___

___ ___ ___ ___ ___ ___ ___ ___ ___

Circle only the capital letters inside the mermaid circle. Then write them, in order, on the blank lines to find out what mermaids are sometimes called.

mermaidS are mythical beIngs that aRe half women and half fish. although numerous sightings havE been made, there is No proof they actually exiSt.

___ ___ ___ ___ ___ ___ of the sea

The Seahorse Merry-Go-Round is a big hit with the mermaids. The tickets sell out right away!

The ride continues, but 10 things have changed. Find and circle them in the picture below.

Follow these easy steps to draw a mermaid.

1

2

3

4

Try it here.

The Little Mermaid is one of the most popular fairy tales. It was first published in 1837. Use the code to find out the name of the author of this famous story.

Follow the tangled paths to find out which seashell each mermaid wants. Write the mermaid's name on the correct line.

Aqua   Kai   Cora   Shelly

_____   _____   _____   _____

Connect the dots to create a best friend for the mermaids.

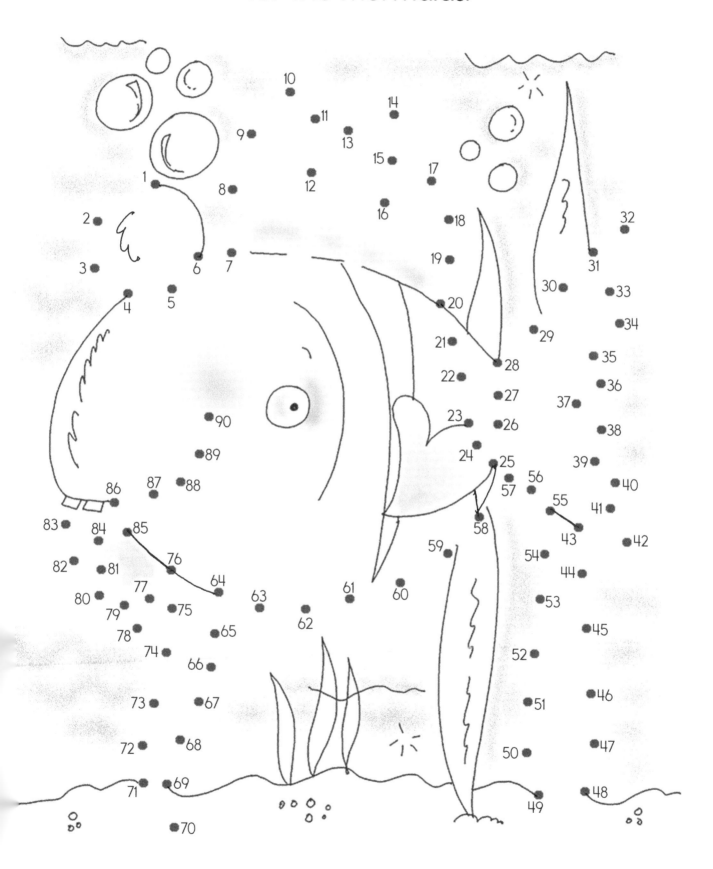

This mermaid has lots of different fish friends!
How many of each kind do you see? Write the
number of each kind of fish in the correct box.

Mermaids call the ocean home. Look up, down, across, and diagonally to find the names of these 10 other creatures that also live under the sea.

jellyfish   seahorse   octopus   lobster

turtle   shark   crab   dolphin

clam   eel

```
c q o k w u n c d l h s
r i b f b i j l q k t h
a c a g h a j a e a e a
b n l p o p q m e j e r
m o l r z c a s h r l k
a o x r h b t s j g a o
d x r u i u i o u k u l
k z a t h f e c p y k o
b x h r y n b g q u j b
p w a l f v h z y t s s
c x l s e a h o r s e t
j e e b z o x x u v z e
j n s d z k y w q c y r
t u r t l e r w v w t i
f j e d z b w k t x j b
```

Circle only the capital letters in the bubble frame. Then write them, in order, on the blank lines to find out the name of a blue-green stone that is treasured by mermaids.

bAck in medieval times the existence of mermaids were never Questioned. people were sUre they lived in the seA aMongst other creAtuRes. nowadays we realIze they are oNly mythical bEings.

___ ___ ___ ___ ___ ___ ___ ___ ___ ___

Many believe that mermaids live in all five oceans.
Use the code cubes to complete some fun
facts about these great bodies of water.

1

O	C	E	A	N
water	largest	ice	circles	third

2

F	A	C	T	S
second	tides	warmest	fish	winter

Atlantic Ocean—
This comes in as the _____ largest of the oceans.
                    2F

It produces the highest _____ anywhere.
                        2A

Southern Ocean—
It includes the area of _____ which
                        1O

_____ around Antarctica.
1A

Indian Ocean—
It is the _____ largest ocean. It has also
          1N

been found to be the _____ .
                     2C

Pacific Ocean—
It is the _____ ocean on Earth. Most of our
          1C

_____ come from here.
2T

Arctic Ocean—
This is the smallest of the
oceans. It's almost completely
covered in _____ during _____ .
           1E   2S

19

Christopher Columbus once recorded that he had spotted three mermaids! Complete each math problem, then match your answer to the letter code and write it on the blank lines to spell out what he probably saw instead.

31 = T
20 = M
18 = A
23 = E
14 = S
46 = N

| 17+3 | 11+7 | 50-4 | 36-18 | 23+8 | 30-7 | 15+8 | 23-9 |

___ ___ ___ ___ ___ ___ ___ ___

Color this picture and the one on the reverse side any way you'd like. Then cut out along the thick outer line and the dashed circle to make a hanger to put over your doorknob.

Color this picture and the one on the reverse side any way you'd like. Then cut out along the thick outer line and the dashed circle to make a hanger to put over your doorknob.

LOVES MERMAIDS!

Find and circle the two mermaids who look exactly like this one. They are identical triplets!

Write the word "mermaid" into the boxes from top to bottom. The letters will finish spelling words that often describe her home, the ocean.

li[ ]itless

aw[ ]some

sto[ ]my

[ ]ighty

w[ ]ves

beaut[ ]ful

[ ]eep

Find and circle the names of 10 popular characters from the Disney movie, *The Little Mermaid*. Look up, down, across, and diagonally.

SEBASTIAN TRITON MAX URSULA ARIEL
ERIC JETSAM SCUTTLE FLOUNDER FLOTSAM

T S D I S E B A S T I A N M
J E T S A M F E B E A N B M
R E M A X R T A R I T L F I
F M L U T Z R F L O T S A M
L E A M A Q I E T R A A U Z
O E R J N A T Y L J J U N S
U T S U R M O A T M L F S U
N T M I D O N E E T A R C F
D N E S A U M R E R E A U A
E L E I I A R U D S R S T R
R R G O T E R S T T I U T X
M R S M L A L M U P C N L T
U H E I O I T O R L T L E I
E L J C R U D A R A A M C K

What do you think this mermaid sees?
Draw it in the open space.

Follow the directions to help this mermaid find a good place to hide from scuba divers. Follow this bubble path...

Quick! Lead the way!

Shade in...

⭐ 4 bubbles down
⭐ 2 bubbles to the right
⭐ 2 bubbles up
⭐ 3 bubbles to the right
⭐ 3 bubbles down
⭐ 5 bubbles to the left
⭐ 3 bubbles down
⭐ 2 bubbles to the right

These underwater musicians are having a jam session.
Bet they sound good!

Take a long look and you'll find that 9 things have changed. Find and circle them.

Look up, down, across, and diagonally to find and circle the word "mermaid" the number of times shown under the waves.

```
O  X  H  F  V  G  J  M  P  U  K  H  M  M  O
M  E  R  M  A  I  D  M  E  B  T  D  B  D  G
Z  N  A  Z  G  X  W  S  L  R  W  Q  I  O  D
M  L  K  E  Q  P  A  A  Y  R  M  A  E  S  S
E  J  M  E  R  M  A  I  D  D  M  A  B  A  H
R  Q  M  E  R  M  A  I  D  R  E  H  I  K  D
M  E  R  M  A  I  D  I  E  V  R  Q  I  D  I
A  T  P  O  L  R  A  M  B  O  M  Y  S  D  A
I  A  M  E  R  M  A  I  D  X  A  V  G  L  M
D  P  O  K  R  M  E  R  M  A  I  D  M  X  R
I  T  V  E  M  E  R  M  A  I  D  A  B  V  E
D  B  M  P  A  D  H  I  U  O  E  B  U  P  M
```

Use the code at the bottom of the page to find the answers to these mermaid riddles.

"And then what?"

What type of phone does a mermaid talk on?

___

___ ___ ___ ___ ___ ___ ___ ___ ___ ___ .

How do mermaids send messages on the internet?

___ ___   ___ ___ ___ ___ ___ ___ ___ .

Starfish Code

 =A

 =S   =H   =L   =P   =H   =O

=B   =N   =I   =Y   =M   =E

31

Write the letter that comes just before the one shown to find out what a mermaid's tail does based on her mood.

__ __ __ __ __ __ __
D   I   B   O   H   F   T

__ __ __ __ __ __
D   P   M   P   S   T

Use the clues to decide which mermaid is having a birthday today. Draw a party hat on her head.

A. She has long hair.
B. She is wearing a necklace.
C. She is holding a large cupcake.

This mermaid needs your help to get the correct answers that will pop the bubbles so she can reach her magic crown. Work out the math problems to find the secret numbers and write them on the blank lines.

Number of days in the month of March

Amount of quarters in a dollar

Number of seconds in a minute

Number of letters in "California"

Number of eggs in a dozen

The next even number that comes after 12

This mermaid is getting her hair done in a new style! Study the picture a few minutes and try to remember the details. Then turn the page and answer the questions.

Can you remember without looking back a page?

1. What kind of creature is behind the mermaid?

_____

2. What pattern is on the mermaid's purse?

_____

3. What is the name of this beauty shop?

_____

4. What is the jellyfish holding?

_____

5. What word is the mermaid thinking?

_____

6. What number is on the mermaid's headband?

_____

7. What is on the back of the mirror?

_____

8. What shape is the mermaid's necklace?

_____

Try playing this memory game with a friend. Write a new question here.

_____

_____

_____

Solutions

page 1

This mermaid is playing a magical tune that signals her ocean friends to come and play. Use the vowels in the bubbles to fill in the names of her special pals.

a e i o u

wh a l e
s e a l
d o l p h i n
st i n g r a y
t u r t l e
l o b s t e r

page 2

Find and circle the one King Neptune that is different from the others.

page 3

Find and circle the hidden heart, thumb, loaf of bread, pineapple, lips, feather duster, sock, ladder, clown hat, and rose.

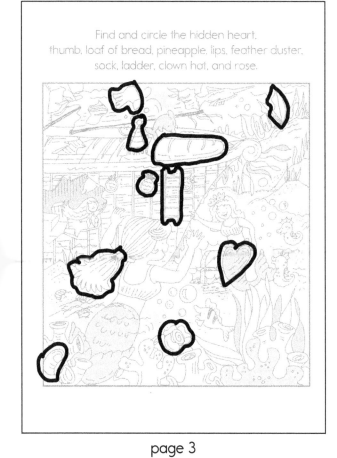

page 4

Use the picture clues to fill in the crossword. Some letters are included to give you a start.

o c t o p u s
c l a m
s e a h o r s e
l o b s t e r
e e l
t u r t l e

Help these kids find their way to the dock to
spot a mermaid before she disappears!

page 5

The first syllable of mermaid is MER, which means "sea"
in what language? Write the letter that comes before
the one shown in each fish to spell the answer.

F R E N C H
G S F O D I

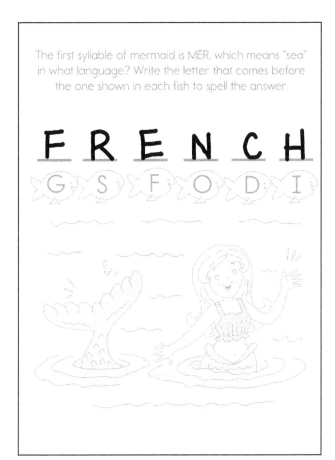

page 7

Write the opposite of each word shown on the left. When
you are done, print the letters in the squares from top to
bottom on the nine blank lines below. They will spell out
the name of a fish with a "heavenly" name.

front— b a c k
huge— t i n y
bad— g o o d
messy— n e a t
short— l o n g
empty— f u l l
mean— n i c e
fast— s l o w
low— h i g h

a n g e l f i s h

page 8

Circle only the capital letters inside the mermaid circle.
Then write them, in order, on the blank lines to find out
what mermaids are sometimes called.

mermaidS are mythical
beings that aRe half
women and half fish.
although numerous
sightings havE been
made, there is No
proof they
actually exiSt.

S I R E N S of the sea

page 9

The ride continues, but 10 things have changed. Find and circle them in the picture below.

page 11

The Little Mermaid is one of the most popular fairy tales. It was first published in 1837. Use the code to find out the name of the author of this famous story.

O = N ☆ = C ▢ = I ▮ = D
● = R △ = H ★ = E ▪ = S
▲ = T ♡ = A

HANS

CHRISTIAN

ANDERSEN

page 13

Follow the tangled paths to find out which seashell each mermaid wants. Write the mermaid's name on the correct line.

Aqua   Kai   Cora   Shelly

Cora   Aqua   Shelly   Kai

page 14

Connect the dots to create a best friend for the mermaids.

page 15

page 16

This mermaid has lots of different fish friends!
How many of each kind do you see? Write the
number of each kind of fish in the correct box.

10

3

4

5

3

page 17

Mermaids call the ocean home. Look up, down,
across, and diagonally to find the names of these
10 other creatures that also live under the sea.

jellyfish   seahorse   octopus   lobster
turtle   shark   crab   dolphin
             clam   eel

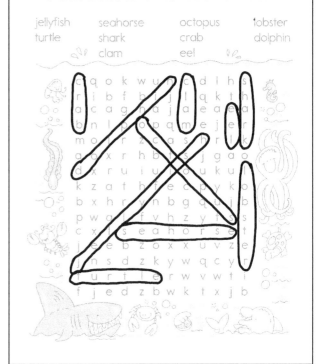

18

Circle only the capital letters in the bubble frame. Then
write them, in order, on the blank lines to find out the name
of a blue-green stone that is treasured by mermaids.

bAck in medieval times the existence
of mermaids were never Questioned.
people were Ure they lived in the seA
aMongst other creAtuRes. nowadays
we realIze they are oNly
mythical bEings.

A Q U A M A R I N E

page 19

Many believe that mermaids live in all five oceans.
Use the code cubes to complete some fun
facts about these great bodies of water.

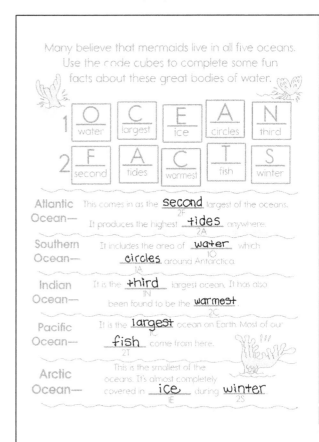

Atlantic Ocean— This comes in as the __second__ largest of the oceans.
It produces the highest __tides__ anywhere.

Southern Ocean— It includes the area of __water__ which __circles__ around Antarctica.

Indian Ocean— It is the __third__ largest ocean. It has also been found to be the __warmest__

Pacific Ocean— It is the __largest__ ocean on Earth. Most of our __fish__ come from here.

Arctic Ocean— This is the smallest of the oceans. It's almost completely covered in __ice__ during __winter__

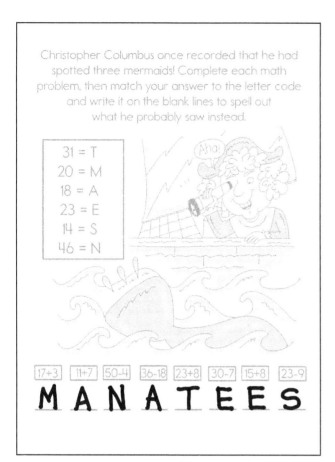

Christopher Columbus once recorded that he had spotted three mermaids! Complete each math problem, then match your answer to the letter code and write it on the blank lines to spell out what he probably saw instead.

| 31 = T |
| 20 = M |
| 18 = A |
| 23 = E |
| 14 = S |
| 46 = N |

Aha!

| 17+3 | 11+7 | 50-4 | 36-18 | 23+8 | 30-7 | 15+8 | 23-9 |

M A N A T E E S

page 20

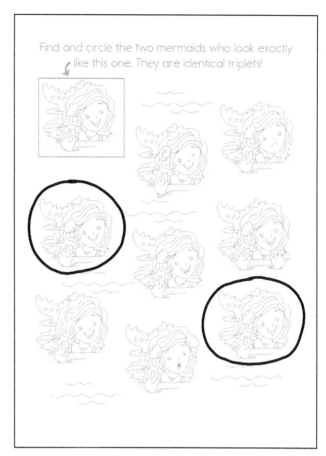

Find and circle the two mermaids who look exactly like this one. They are identical triplets!

page 23

Write the word "mermaid" into the boxes from top to bottom. The letters will finish spelling words that often describe her home, the ocean.

li **m** itless
awe **e** some
sto **r** my
m ighty
w **a** ves
beautif **i** ul
d eep

page 24

Find and circle the names of 10 popular characters from the Disney movie, *The Little Mermaid*. Look up, down, across, and diagonally.

SEBASTIAN TRITON MAX URSULA ARIEL
ERIC JETSAM SCUTTLE FLOUNDER FLOTSAM

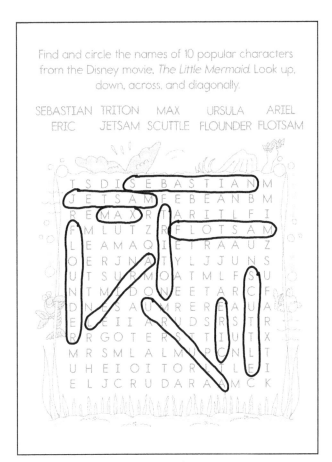

Follow the directions to help this mermaid find a good place to hide from scuba divers. Follow this bubble path...

Shade in...
☆ 4 bubbles down
☆ 2 bubbles to the right
☆ 2 bubbles up
☆ 3 bubbles to the right
☆ 3 bubbles down
☆ 5 bubbles to the left
☆ 3 bubbles down
☆ 2 bubbles to the right

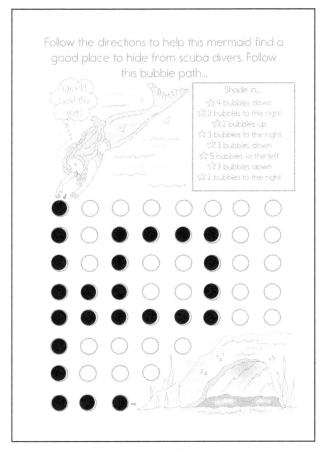

Take a long look and you'll find that 9 things have changed. Find and circle them.

Look up, down, across, and diagonally to find and circle the word "mermaid" the number of times shown under the waves.

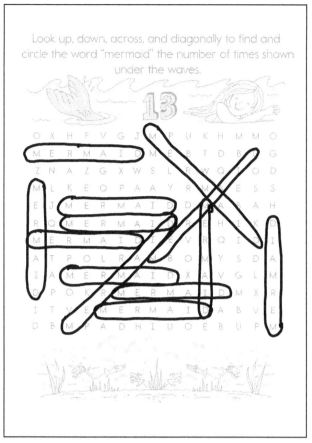

Use the code at the bottom of the page to find the answers to these mermaid riddles.

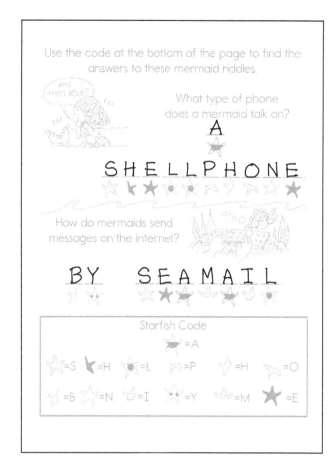

What type of phone does a mermaid talk on?

A

SHELLPHONE

How do mermaids send messages on the internet?

BY SEAMAIL

Starfish Code

= A

=S =H =L =P =H =O

=B =N =I =Y =M =E

Write the letter that comes just before the one shown to find out what a mermaid's tail does based on her mood.

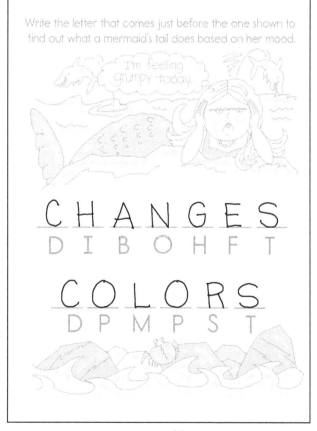

I'm feeling grumpy today.

CHANGES
D I B O H F T

COLORS
D P M P S T

Use the clues to decide which mermaid is having a birthday today. Draw a party hat on her head.

A. She has long hair.
B. She is wearing a necklace.
C. She is holding a large cupcake.

page 33

This mermaid needs your help to get the correct answers that will pop the bubbles so she can reach her magic crown. Work out the math problems to find the secret numbers and write them on the blank lines.

Amount of quarters in a dollar — 4

Number of days in the month of March — 31

Number of seconds in a minute — 60

Number of letters in "California" — 10

Number of eggs in a dozen — 12

The next even number that comes after 12 — 14

page 34

Can you remember without looking back a page?

1. What kind of creature is behind the mermaid?
shark

2. What pattern is on the mermaid's purse?
hearts

3. What is the name of this beauty shop?
Sea Spray Salon

4. What is the jellyfish holding?
shampoo

5. What word is the mermaid thinking?
No!

6. What number is on the mermaid's headband?
2

7. What is on the back of the mirror?
flower

8. What shape is the mermaid's necklace?
triangle

Try playing this memory game with a friend. Write a new question here.

page 36

46